I0527177

Edward C. Hegeler, First National Bank

A Protest Against the Supreme Court of Illinois

and also against its legal and moral doctrine as expressed in and

illustrated in connection with the case of Edward C. Hegeler vs. The First

National Bank of Peru

Edward C. Hegeler, First National Bank

A Protest Against the Supreme Court of Illinois
*and also against its legal and moral doctrine as expressed in and illustrated in
connection with the case of Edward C. Hegeler vs. The First National Bank of Peru*

ISBN/EAN: 9783337382995

Printed in Europe, USA, Canada, Australia, Japan

Cover: Foto ©Andreas Hilbeck / pixelio.de

More available books at **www.hansebooks.com**

A PROTEST

AGAINST THE

SUPREME COURT

OF

ILLINOIS,

AND ALSO AGAINST ITS LEGAL AND MORAL DOCTRINE

AS EXPRESSED IN AND ILLUSTRATED IN CONNECTION WITH THE CASE OF

EDWARD C. HEGELER
vs.
THE FIRST NATIONAL BANK OF PERU. }

Reported in Illinois Report.
Vol. 129, Page 157.

BY THE PLAINTIFF IN THE CASE.

CHICAGO :
THE OPEN COURT PUBLISHING CO.
1890.

My objects in publishing this pamphlet are public as well as personal :

Firstly—The Supreme Court has insinuated a charge against me in deciding the case entitled "Edward C. Hegeler against the First National Bank of Peru," (vol. 129 Illinois Reports, page 157) which I must not suffer to pass unrepelled and whose groundlessness and sophistry I must expose. I owe it to my present and future good name and to my family to· correct the misinformation and misrepresentation that asperses my conduct and reputation in connection with the case in view.

It devolves upon me not only to manifest the absolute groundlessness of such charge, but also to express the disdain that I properly and naturally feel for those who assail my honor.

Secondly—It seems to me a duty I owe to the public to expose the delinquencies of the tribunal that is capable of needlessly and falsely visiting upon those suitors that are compelled to appeal to it for justice the burden of imputations that are unmerited and that infringe upon their unsullied characters.

Thirdly—I deem it proper and of urgent need that certain doctrines and standards of law and morals that receive the sanction of our highest judicial tribunal, should be openly discussed, to the end that the public may understand their debased character and the moral incompetence of those who sustain them.

THE CASE—PRELIMINARY.

On Dec. 22nd, 1882, the De Steiger Glass Company—a corporation of La Salle, Illinois, whose capital stock was $50,000—had been carrying on for several years at that place an extensive glass manfacturing business and had made most of its deposits with and transacted most of its financial affairs through the First National Bank of Peru.

On the date mentioned above the bank caused to be entered up against the glass company, in favor of the bank, in the Circuit Court of La Salle county, Illinois, upon corre-

I credited this showing, and according to it the total liabilities of the company were $40,660, part of which, viz., the window-house mortgage of $5,000, I was to refund for a longer period, leaving a floating indebtedness of $35,660. Against this the assets showed material and stock partly specified in "Exhibit C" and bills receivable of $33,550, so that the real estate outside of the window-house mortgage (which was a separate part of the plant of secondary importance) was wholly available as unincumbered assets over and above liabilities to within $2,110 of its value. I was convinced that whatever embarrassments the glass company was suffering were due solely to its lack of a sufficient working capital and that the, proposed loan of ten thousand dollars by me would very scantily supply that need. The subject of security for my proposed loan arising, the effect upon the credit of the glass company of a mortgage in my favor was discussed, and the prejudice which the giving of a mortgage (even if small) on its property by a business concern is apt to excite. The supposition of a non-recorded mortgage was mentioned here and I told Mr. De Steiger that I did not want such a mortgage, because I regarded such course as dishonest against the public. And I then suggested to Mr. De Steiger that his proper way was to negotiate a loan from somebody to the amount of forty or fifty thousand dollars by mortgage on the plant so as to make the company independent of credit and do a cash business.

As, however, such a measure would require considerable time to consummate and as the glass company represented its needs as immediate, the discussion relating to a large loan by a mortgage on the entire plant was only incidental. Therefore, in conclusion of our negotiations and in full faith in the representations made to me by the glass company of its financial condition, I loaned to it the ten thousand dollars, taking only the ordinary notes of the glass company endorsed by the members of the De Steiger family, who were apparently its officers and principal stockholders, and who, according to Mr. De Steiger's statement "Exhibit C," had still an unsettled estate amounting to $35,000 which belonged to the De Steiger family, equal shares among five. These notes were three in number, all of them dated September 21st, 1882. Two of them were each for the sum of $2,500, due severally and respectively in six and twelve months after date. The third note was for the sum of $5,000, due eighteen months after date. Each of them was endorsed in guarantee of the payment of the same by Phil R. De Steiger, E. A. De Steiger, A. F. De Steiger, J. L. De Steiger, W. F. Modes, Chas. C. Modes, George Modes, and May E. Burton.

In view of the expedient advised by me of raising an ample working capital for the glass company by a large loan on its entire plant, and as, by the statements, the company would still have to carry a floating indebtedness of $25,660 after receiving the desired loan from me, I required of the glass company as one of the conditions of my $10,000 loan a written promise by it that in case it made resort to a mortgage on its property it would give me a first mortgage. The document expressing this promise obtained in my suit the designation "Exhibit L." The fac-simile following this page is a photographic copy of the same, viz. :

Again on November 20th, 1882, the glass company, through its same officer, asked for assistance by way of a temporary loan, and I advanced to it the further sum of $4,500 for twenty days against its plain note, and I renewed this note for another twenty days on December 9th, 1882, only thirteen days before the seizure of the whole visible property of the glass company. The renewal of this note was guaranteed by the same endorsers as before, but as to the original I do not recollect.

Now instead of exposing to me its real financial condition at the time of its application for the loan of ten thousand dollars, and instead of having no other liabilities outside of those stated in "Exhibit C" (see p. 4), and instead of being liable to the Peru Bank in only the sum of $4,300 (see p. 4) and to others outside of the window-house mortgage in the aggregate sum of $31,360 (see p. 4), the glass company was at that time liable to the bank in upwards of the sum of $40,000, and so had been and unable to pay any considerable part of the same for upwards of eight months prior thereto. At the time of the trial the bank presented an additional claim of over $17,000, making its whole claim upwards of $57,000.

It was also hopelessly insolvent, owing debts which it was

E. C. HEGELER, Pres't.   OFFICE OF   F. W. MATTHIESSEN, Sec'y

MATTHIESSEN & HEGELER ZINC CO.

SMELTERS OF SPELTER,
AND
MANUFACTURERS OF SHEET ZINC.

La Salle, Ill Sept 21st 1882

We the undersigned, having this day received a
loan of Ten Thousand Dollars from E. C. Hegeler
for which we have given him our notes to
that amount, hereby bind ourselves unto him
that we will not mortgage our bottle glass works
and Window glass works to anyone except him
during the time that the notes remain unpaid,
unless giving him a first mortgage, for the
amount due. And we also bind ourselves
not to sell the above glass works or any
material part thereof during such time. We
also agree to have fire insurance on our
property to the amount of Ten Thousand Dollars
transferred to him and keep same up for
his benefit

D. Sturgis Glass Co.
Phil, N. R. & Sturgis Pres.

unable to pay, besides its liabilities to the bank, to at least an amount equal to the amount of its bank liabilities.

Moreover, and very notable in its relations to my case, the glass company had more than eight months prior to the time of its obtaining my loan of $10,000, viz., on January 10th, 1882, executed and given to the bank the two judgment notes above referred to (see p. 4), upon which the above-mentioned judgments in favor of the bank (see p. 4), were entered; and the same were then at the time of the application of the glass company to me lying hid in the hands of the bank, ready and about to issue for the purpose of transferring the entire visible estate of the glass company to the sole benefit of the bank.

Thus the means by which the glass company obtained from me my money was fraud of the most conspicuous sort.

At once, upon the entry of the above judgments by con-fession in favor of the bank, it was perceived that proceedings were begun which, in the natural course, must operate to trans-fer to the benefit of the bank alone the entire visible estate of the glass company, and by necessary consequence must defeat all attempts by the unsecured creditors to obtain payment of their dues.

Surprised and vigilant inquiry was naturally provoked into the business history of the glass company and especially into the relations and transactions between it and the bank.

It was ultimately discovered that they were of a very peculiar description, as follows, viz. :

THE CASE AS TO THE BANK.

The First National Bank of Peru was organized under the National Banking Law, with a capital of $100,000. At the time of the transactions here referred to, Theron D. Brewster was its President and Robert V. Sutherland was its Cashier. It employed regularly as its Attorney and Counsel Judge G. S. Eldredge.

The glass company began doing business with the bank about January 1, 1879.

As early at least as the summer of 1880 the bank was noti-fied that the glass company was in need; for it failed to meet its notes and obtained from the bank extensions.

This need grew rapidly during the rest of 1880 and in 1881.

By the National Banking Law all banks organized under it are forbidden to loan to any single corporation an amount greater than ten per cent of the capital of the bank, which percentage in this case was $10,000. Still, in spite of this mandate, and during the latter part of 1880 and the first part of 1881, the bank had very largely over-loaned to the glass company this legal limit; and whatever may have been its anxieties besides, it was specially anxious to conceal its fault from the National Bank Examiner, who made his visit to the bank in December.

Having already in its hands more than $10,000 worth of the delinquent paper of the glass company, a very large amount of which had been from nine months to over a year over-due, the bank during the period from about the middle of August, 1881, to about the middle of December in the same year, ostensibly loaned to the glass company over $30,000 by way of apparent discounts of one note and thirty drafts accepted respectively by one or the other of various parties.

The quality of this paper can be judged by reference to the remarks of the Circuit Court Judge in his decision of my suit, viz.: "Geer was the only one of the acceptors who was "a business man, and in a business requiring such a product "as the glass company made. Burton was a brother-in-law of "De Steiger and was a laborer in the glass company's works, "and Munn was a lawyer in Chicago and not a customer of "the glass company.

"It further appears in evidence that Phil. R. De Steiger "told another member of his company that this was sham and "worthless paper and that Sutherland the Cashier knew it ; but "the glass company had got into the bank so deep that it "could not help itself, and that Sutherland required these "deceptive acceptances to be renewed from time to time to "deceive the bank examiner.".

None of this paper was ever paid by the acceptors or by the glass company, but as it fell due it was renewed from time to time by the bank. The bank was well aware of the character of this paper, for it discounted large amounts of it after the acceptors had failed to pay former acceptances and also even took no pains to send other large amounts to the acceptors for collection. Mr. Brewster, the President of the bank, admitted in his testimony in my suit that he understood that the glass company was really getting its capital from the bank.

By the 10th day of January, 1882, over $13,000 of these acceptances had become due and delinquent and the rest amounting to over $17,000 were morally sure to follow in the same course, as indeed eventually proved to be the case.

The glass company was also liable to the bank on other paper, so as to make an aggregate liability of about $55,000.

About $16,000 of this other paper was considered to have no other value than that lent to it by the credit of the glass company.

In this situation the glass company proposed to give a mortgage on its entire plant as security for the liabilities of the glass company to the bank, the same to stand also as security to Dr. Corbus, who was endorser on about $8,000 of the same paper, as well as an endorser on paper of the glass company for about $5,000 at Freeport. This proposition was made at a meeting, held at the bank over the situation, on the above date, January 10, 1882. There were present at this meeting Phil. R. De Steiger, the President of the glass company, Dr. Corbus and the President of the bank (Mr. Brewster), its Cashier (Mr. Sutherland), and its Attorney (G. S. Eldredge).

Mr. De Steiger, himself, on behalf of the glass company, at once and spontaneously, offered to give the wholesale mortgage. He came to the meeting with Dr. Corbus, his endorser, fully expecting that that measure would be exacted of the glass company by all interested. But it was the bank that demurred and, after private consultation with its lawyer, objected to this. It was the bank that manifested special concern for the credit of the glass company, and thrust forward that argument against the giving of the mortgage. Its officers testify in my suit to that effect. Mr. Brewster, the President of the bank, testifies: " He " (that is De Steiger) " came in in a few days with Dr. Corbus and said he came to " give us security and also Dr. Corbus on the paper he was on " at Freeport, that he wanted to give a mortgage on his prop- " erty. We consulted about that and finally we told him that "if we took a mortgage, putting it on record might affect their "credit. I went back and talked with Judge Eldredge, and the "officers of the bank thought best to take a judgment note "instead of a mortgage."

"It was for our interest to have them continue." " I agreed that we would try to keep them along."

And on cross examination:

Q. "And it was first proposed that a mortgage should be given. Who made that proposition?"

A. "Phil R. De Steiger."

Q. "Who raised the objection to giving a mortgage?"

A. "I think Judge Eldredge raised the objection to giving a mortgage."

Q. "You said something about placing a mortgage on record would hurt or destroy their credit." "What was it you said on that subject?"

A. "I said that; that I thought it would, if we took a mortgage, meaning if we took a mortgage that effect would follow. To put it on record would injure their credit."

Q. "And you thought if you took a mortgage putting it on record would ruin their credit?"

A. "Yes sir."

Q. "And that was the reason then why you did not take a mortgage at the time?"

A. "That was one of the reasons ; yes, sir."

Q. "And in lieu of the mortgage and putting it on record you took this judgment note of $35,000 and kept that in your safe?"

A. "Yes, sir."

Q. "That did not appear in any manner upon your books?"

A. "No, sir."

And Mr. Sutherland, the Cashier of the bank, testified:

"Philip De Steiger first suggested giving a mortgage at "the meeting January 10, 1882, and I, Mr. Brewster, and Judge "Eldredge objected because we were afraid it would injure the "credit of the glass company."

Q. "You thought that the taking of a mortgage of $35,000 and putting it on record that that would be publishing to the world the condition of their accounts with you and the amount of their obligations to you and it would injure their credit?"

A. " Yes, sir."

Q. " And, therefore, instead of taking a mortgage and putting it on record, you took the judgment note of $35,000?"

A. " Yes, sir. Mr. Phil. R. De Steiger said at the time that we have the total indebtedness of the glass company except such as might have been contracted on account of workmen and material used there in the factory. I supposed at the time he was telling the truth."

That the glass company represented at the meeting of January 10, 1882, that it had no considerable indebtedness beyond the liabilities in which the bank was interested except for labor and material, was also testified to by Mr. Brewster, the bank President, who also testified that he then believed the same.

So, not according to the purposes of the glass company as it had projected them, but upon the potent persuasions of the bank prompted solely by concern for its own interests, it was tacitly agreed (that is, for reciprocal considerations, mutual assent or coalescence of minds to the same set of executive doings was mutually affected) between the bank and the glass company that the glass company instead of virtually going into liquidation should continue in business ; that the 'credit of the mutually-recognized-as-insolvent and credit-worthless glass company should be supported and fostered as to others ; that as means to that end no mortgage as proposed should be given, but in lieu thereof that the entire substance of the glass company should be so put into the power of the bank by judgment notes, that while others should be led to believe that good recourse was available for their present and prospective credits on the property of the glass company that belief should always prove disappointed ; that as further means to the same end the existence of such judgment notes should be concealed by the bank, and the glass company allowed to retain the apparent full control of its property as free to the recourse of other present and prospective creditors ; that the bank should further financially assist the glass company, and that the glass company should in the present and future prefer the bank over its other present and future creditors and govern its conduct accordingly.

This expedient of taking wholesale judgment notes in place of other security, so proposed by Judge Eldredge, the lawyer of the bank, was the natural advice of a practitioner who based his advice upon the former decisions of the Supreme Court.

Pursuant to the agreement thus effected the two judgment notes were delivered and carefully concealed. One of them had been given in the usual way of the business of the bank on December 24, 1881, and was for the sum of $5,200 due ten days after date. To this was appended, at the time of the meeting above stated, a warrant of attorney to confess judgment at any time.

The other was a regular judgment note for $35,000 dated January 10th, 1882, and due one day after date.

This done the respective parties to the agreement proceeded to further carry out its stipulations and effected the complete concealment of the judgment notes, the apparent full control by the glass company of its property as free to recourse, the obtaining by it of credit, the continuance of its business until the entry of said judgments, the preferment of the bank, and all the other purposes proposed to be attained by it.

From February 23, 1882 to March 9, 1882, the glass company had an apparent balance to its credit on the regular books of the bank of nearly $8,000.

Yet, although the $5,200 note was overdue, the bank contrary to its otherwise universal custom and without any excuse did not require the note to be taken up. Also, from about July 12, 1882, till the time of the entry of the judgments, the bank cashed the checks of the glass company and instead of entering them all on the books regarded some as cash and carried them along increasing in amount from day to day until at the time of the entry of the judgments these amounted to over $10,000, and upon them, and perhaps some other claims, a further judgment against the glass company in favor of the bank was rendered for upwards of $17,000.

Besides its debt to me the glass company between January 10th, 1882, and the time of the entry of the judgments contracted debts to others in large amounts.

THE SUIT AND PROCEEDINGS THEREIN.

At the time when the bank entered up its judgments against the glass company none of my notes were due, but upon my demand therefor the glass company gave to me on Dec. 30, 1882, a judgment note for the amount owing to me, $14,500, and on the next day I had judgment in my favor entered up and execution issued and levied on the glass company's plant.

As I was, perhaps, the largest unsecured creditor, I filed my bill in equity against the bank in the interest of all the creditors as well as myself, and to the best of my advice and ability prosecuted the suit thus begun through the different grades of the courts as long as any legal resource was available. As the case was decided against me in the Circuit Court on the basis of the former decisions of the Supreme Court regarding judgment notes, I desired to prosecute the matter in the Appellate and Supreme Courts still in the interest of all creditors who would join with me.

However, this representation by me on appeal of other creditors had to be abandoned on the advice of my lawyer that it was impracticable.

In every stage of the proceedings under my bill the critical and controlling question has been, as of course I was well aware it would be, the question of fraud, the question of whether or not the relations and transactions between the bank and the glass company, morally fraudulent, were legally so.

I was aware to some extent of the narrowing influence that the habitual recourse to precedents rather than to principles admittedly exercises upon the decisions of courts of law, especially those of lower rank, and so I was prepared to sustain without surprise whatever disappointments might be in store for me by the action of the lower courts, but I strongly hoped and expected that the Supreme Court would deal with the question of law involved in my case in a spirit that would recognize its importance.

Indeed, I thought myself warranted in expecting from the Supreme Court a marshalling and critical study of the precedents as related to the underlying principles which the precedents are supposed to exemplify.

I believed that such a mode of treatment would lead them to perceive that the business and ethical standards of modern life demand an application of fundamental principles in such a way as still to operate to defeat all the devices of fraud.

THE LEADING ALLEGATIONS OF THE BILL.

The bill of complaint set out the facts and circumstances heretofore recited at large, and as the gist of its import made averments as follows, viz.:—

"That although the notes upon which said judgments were confessed in favor of the Peru Bank were dated anterior to the time when the indebtedness for which said judgments were confessed was contracted, still said notes were kept by said bank in its custody and concealed from the knowledge of complainant, and the judgments thereon were confessed after said glass company became indebted to complainant. That it is inequitable and unjust for said bank to assert a lien upon said premises under said judgments as against complainant."

"Your orator would further represent that, although said judgments in favor of the First National Bank of Peru were not entered up until December 22, 1882, yet said notes both became due in January, 1882, and were each accompanied by power of attorney to confess judgment at any time; that prior to January 10, 1882, the date of execution of each of said powers of attorney, the De Steiger Glass Company was unable to meet its obligations, and was insolvent, which was then, and prior thereto, known by said First National Bank of Peru; that said bank had cause for so believing; that just prior thereto said glass company offered to mortgage its property to said bank, but said bank refused, because it would injure the credit of the glass company and prevent it from obtaining elsewhere further credits and loans; that thereupon said bank took from said glass company said notes and powers of attorney attached thereto, and *agreed to conceal the same and to allow said glass company to retain the full control of the property free from any recorded or known lien; that in pursuance of such agreement* said First National Bank of Peru, with the intention of allowing said glass company to obtain new and future credit elsewhere and to defraud its creditors, *did keep concealed* in its possession for over eleven months, and until December 22, 1882, said judgment notes, when it entered judgment thereon and took out executions and made levies as aforesaid, with the express purpose of defeating the just claims of your orator and other creditors of said glass company incurred during the period of said concealment, and concealed the amount of indebtedness from the glass company to it until December 22, 1882.''

"That your orator advanced $10,000 Sept. 21, 1882, and $4,500 Nov. 20, 1882, on the false and fraudulent statements of the De Steiger Glass Company as to its financial condition, and upon the delusive and fictitious credit given it by said First National Bank of Peru in allowing it to retain all its property apparently free from incumbrance, and that had your orator known or suspected the existence of said judgment notes, he would have given no credits or loans whatever to said glass company; that such concealment enabled the glass company, under the semblance of being the owner of a large amount of unincumbered real estate and personal property, to deceive and mislead your orator and other persons to give it credit that would otherwise have been withheld, by reason of which said glass company did contract the aforesaid debts to your orator, now remaining wholly unpaid.''

Voluminous testimony was taken, all of which was supposed to be relevant to the allegations of the bill of complaint, and in November, 1886, the case was tried in the La Salle Circuit Court. From that Court appeals were taken first to the Appellate Court and then to the Supreme Court of Illinois.

While my case was pending in the Supreme Court, Mr. E. F. Bull, my senior counsel, who had had the chief management of my suit and who alone was at the time fitly familiar with the points of law and fact involved, died, and the conduct of the suit fell upon his surviving partner, Mr. Strawn, who was comparatively uninformed regarding it.

On March 5, 1889, Mr. Strawn, in forwarding to me a copy of the brief on my behalf that he was to file on the morrow of that day, informed me that the other side would now file their brief, after which I would have an opportunity to file a reply brief to whatever should appear to require it in the brief of the other side.

The brief of the bank was forwarded by mail on March 13, 1889. On the next day but one I wrote to Mr. Strawn, saying:

"I received appellee's brief and I wish an answer to be given to the remarks of counsel on pages 27 and 28.''

These "remarks" were an impertinent and groundless *ad hominem* argument appended by Judge Eldredge, the lawyer of the bank, to the main body of the suggestions of his brief. Referring to "Exhibit L" and the circumstances under which it was given, he went on to argue or rather insinuate that I had done just as the bank had, and he concluded by saying:

"So it will be seen that this loan was made upon the ex-"press stipulation that he (Hegeler) should have the first "lien by way of a mortgage on the property of the De Steiger "Glass Company *when the exigency should occur for its execu-* "*tion.*"

Thus he insinuated that I was in collusion with the glass company in the same way as was the bank.

At the time of the trial of my case in the Circuit Court the counsel for the bank and for the glass company had made an effort to produce an impression to this same effect and had entirely failed therein. This had also been repeated in the Appellate Court.

On the next day I received a letter from Mr. Strawn, saying:

" Your case with the Peru Bank has been called and taken under advisement by the Supreme Court and the time for further argument is closed."

It thus occurred that the sophistries as to my conduct insinuated into my case by the lawyer for the bank were not immediately answered and resented.

In June, 1889, the Supreme Court filed their opinion adverse to my contention.

After reciting the allegations of my bill (see p. 14) as the sole ground on which I expected to prevail they declare as follows, viz.:—"It must be admitted that if the averment that ",appellee '*agreed to conceal the same, and to allow said glass* "*company to retain the full control of the property, free from* " *any recorded or known lien, and that in pursuance of such* "*agreement it did conceal,*' etc., was stricken out of the bill, it " would be demurrable for want of equity appearing in its face " Field et al. *vs.* Ridgley et al., 116 Ill., 424."

"There is not a particle of evidence in the record to support that averment."

It would naturally seem that when a court has concluded that there is *no proof whatever* of the controlling facts of a case, they were supplied with the very best possible grounds for dismissing it.

But evidently such grounds were not sufficient for the Illinois Supreme Court in my case, for they virtually proceed to imply that my own counsel were aware of the utter groundlessness of the controlling averment and that in arguing the case my counsel virtually confessed a total failure of proof in its support. They go on as follows, viz.:

"There is not a particle of evidence in the record to support that averment, nor is it relied upon in the argument as being essential to complainant's cause. On the contrary, the argument proceeds throughout upon the proposition that the bank took its notes and held them under *circumstances* that made its conduct operate as a fraud upon others. There is no pretense that there was any agreement to conceal its claim against the glass company, much less that any such agreement was made for the purpose of enabling the company to obtain credit from others. No evidence can be found in the record proving or tending to prove acts or declarations on the part of appellee calculated to induce. appellant to give credit to the glass company."

Considering that a mere reference to the record in the case and to the printed briefs and arguments of my counsel is all that is needed for the flat disproof of these wholesale declarations we may say that the same ought to be at least astonishing.

The averment in question *was precisely* the very gist of our reliance. In all stages of my case *it was pretended* by all means that the bank agreed to conceal its claim against the glass company and for the purpose of enabling the company to obtain credit from others.

In proof of this I will give some decisive quotations from the brief filed by my counsel in the case.

After printing in full the controlling allegations as they are hereinbefore printed (pp. 14-15) the brief goes on :

" If. these allegations are sufficient in equity to authorize "the relief prayed for then the decree must be reversed, for " *they have been clearly and conclusively proved,* 'and that too by " evidence of the officers of the bank."

Appellant's Brief p. 6.

" The bank took the judgment notes upon which these "judgments were entered and held *and concealed,* the same un-" der circumstances that made their conduct operate as a fraud " upon others."   Appellant's Brief, p. 15.

" The best way in the opinion of the bank officers to real-"ize on the capital invested was to continue the business of " the glass company in hopes that . it would weather the "storm."   Appellant's· Brief, p. 38.

" Why did the bank desire to·sustain its " (the glass company's) " credit ?"

" For no other purpose than to enable it to borrow money "and get advances from others."   Appellant's Brief, p. 39.

But it is needless to quote further. The whole argument in pp. 35 to 42 of Appellant's Brief, is to no other intent or. purpose but to insist that the .bank agreed to conceal and allow the glass company to manage their property as free from liens for the very purpose of enabling it to obtain credit and money from others.

MY PETITION FOR A REHEARING.

But the Supreme Court in its original opinion, not content with declaring that I had utterly failed to prove whatever case could be deemed as stated in my bill and implying for my counsel a lack of comprehension of the points of the case, yet as though troubled with misgivings in spite of its sweeping declarations, seemed to grasp for support at the impertinent counter attack upon me made by the lawyer of the bank, and said :

" Months after the transaction between appellee and the company, appellant, according to his own testimony, declined, or at least consented not to take mortgage security, because it would ' spoil their credit.' He refused to take a mortgage and withhold it from record, because he thought that would ' be dishonest against the public,' but he was willing to and did make an agreement with Mr. De Steiger that, in case the company desired to give a mortgage he should be notified and have a first mortgage. It would certainly be difficult to condemn the transaction between appellee and the glass company without also pronouncing that of appellant fraudulent (and he is the only one here complaining); but we know of no rule of law or business which condemns either."

It was evident upon the reading of the opinion of the Supreme Court that the judges themselves had slighted the points of the case. They had failed to examine the circumstances under which I made my loan, shown in Exhibits "C" and "D," the written statement from De Steiger's memory and the balance sheet furnished to me by the glass company. Though I hold that a court of justice should not pronounce imputations upon the character of any suitor without the most careful examination of the testimony, and that a court forgets its dignity when it pronounces in the form of insinuations what it does not dare to pronounce direct; I had to recognize as an excuse for its conduct that they supposed from the neglect to repel the insinuations of the lawyer of the bank in my reply brief, either that I admitted the same or that I was insensible to them, and that they also might follow the same methods unchallenged. But I still felt faith enough in the Supreme Court and in their regard for judicial ethics to expect that when they should be informed of the true state of the testimony and of my sensitive regard for my good name, they would absolutely withdraw the personally injurious part of the opinion, and also reconsider the whole case.

With this view the following petition for rehearing was prepared for me by my friend and counsel, Gen. M. M. Trumbull. Mr. Strawn, the former partner of Mr. Bull, also lent his assistance at the close. Parts having no reference to the present issue are omitted. By the rules of the Supreme Court no argument is allowed on petitions for rehearing, but the same must be sustained, if at all, by the bare statement of points.

PETITION FOR REHEARING.

MAY IT PLEASE THE COURT:

The appellant, Edward C. Hegeler, respectfully asks a rehearing of this cause, for the reason, amongst others, that important evidence, appearing in the full report of the testimony and favorable to appellant, was not presented to the Supreme Court; that the absence of this testimony was not due to any fault of appellant; that by reason of the absence of this testimony the Supreme Court was misled to an opinion, contrary, as appellant believes, to that which would have resulted from an examination of the full testimony, had it been presented to the court; that by reason of this incomplete presentation of the evidence the court was led to draw a parallel between the actions of appellant and appellee injurious to appellant, and which appellant believes the court would not have drawn had the full testimony been presented. This testimony, appellant believes, was omitted from the Abstract by appellant's counsel, now deceased, under the belief that the unjust insinuation made by appellee and disproved by such testimony, would not be repeated. Appellant had no part in preparing the Abstract. For this and other reasons appellant asks that he may be permitted to present some points for the information of the court, believing that a correct understanding of the evidence, in connection with all the attendant circumstances, will procure a reversal of the decree, and a justification by the court of appellant's motives and action in the matters investigated and adjudicated in this cause.

I.

Presentation of points in support of appellant's petition for a rehearing in the matter of conclusions drawn by the court in the following portion of the opinion filed in the case:

" There is nothing in the bill, and certainly nothing in the evidence, to show that at the time appellee took its notes and

(Petition for Rehearing, continued.)

refused to take mortgage security'it did not honestly believe, that notwithstanding the insolvency of the glass company, it would, if its credit could be maintained, successfully recover from its embarrassment; continue business and pay all its debt:s."

1.   Although there may be very little verbal testimony to contradict that part of the opinion, the circumstantial evidence tends the other way.   It shows that, although the bank may have had a hope that the glass company might recover, it had no belief in it, because, ·

2.   At the time the bank declined a mortgage, it required and received a judgment note for. $35,000, a far better security for the bank than a mortgage.

3.   This judgment note was kept concealed from the bank examiner, and from everybody else.   It was held by the bank as a secret lien in its own favor, and against all other creditors of the glass company.

4.   The evidence all tends to show that at the time referred to the bank had far more doubt as to the survival of the glass company than belief in it.

5.   It is evident that the bank knew at the time it took the secret lien that the De Steiger Glass Company was a financial wreck.   The record shows that the bank officers knew they were carrying more than $40,000 of bogus drafts drawn by the glass company upon men who were notoriously irresponsible.   For instance, drafts to the amount of nearly $10,000 upon employés who worked packing bottles in the packing house, saloon keepers of no responsibility, and similar men of straw.

6.   And, in addition, the record shows that from the time this $35,000 note was given in January until the following June, this fictitious paper long past due, and not protested, was not renewed, and was renewed in June not because the bank thought it *bona fide* paper, but in order to deceive the bank examiner who was expected to examine the bank in July.

7.   The bank took a secret lien, both to enable the glass company to recover from its embarrassment, and to prolong its own life.   It was clear that a mortgage of $40,000 to the bank

would close the bank. Taking judgments for $5,325, $35 050 and $18,139.46 did close the bank. The bank must have known it was doomed, and took its secret lien to enable it to strike at a more favorable opportunity.

II.

Presentation of points in support of appellant's petition for a rehearing in the matter of the conclusions drawn by the court in the following portion of the opinion:

"Months after the transaction between appellee and the Glass Company, appellant, according to his own testimony, declined, or at least consented not to take mortgage security, because it would 'spoil their credit.'"

1. The evidence proves that this was the true reason. A mortgage for a small amount on a manufacturer's works will destroy his credit, as it shows that he can not raise the money in any other way and that some creditors are afraid. The refusal was against appellant's own interest, and in the interest of the glass company and all its creditors.

2. It was not the true reason why the bank refused a mortgage. The true reason was concealment of the large debt. It already had large sums of money in jeopardy through its advances to the glass company, sums far beyond the legal limit. Its own interests had become identified with the continuance of the glass works. It risked nothing. Appellant risked his money, not as an act of business but friendliness, and he took equal chances with everybody else.

3. A mortgage taken by the bank would have been more dangerous to the credit of the bank than to that of the glass company. It would have exposed its imprudent and illegitimate methods of business.

III.

Presentation of points in support of appellant's petition for a rehearing in the matter of the conclusion drawn by the court in the following portion of the opinion:

"He refused to take a mortgage and withhold it from record, because he thought that would be 'dishonest against

(Petition for Rehearing, continued.)

the public,' but he was willing to and did make an agreement with Mr. De Steiger, that in case the company desired to give a mortgage, he should be notified and have a first mortgage.''

1. This part of the opinion intimates that the acts of appellant in this particular are not consistent with the reasons given by him, and readers of the opinion might construe them as a charge that appellant had been guilty of insincerity or hypocrisy, a charge which the court could hardly have intended to make, and which is disproved by every portion of the evidence.

The agreement, '' Exhibit L,'' is as follows :.

LA SALLE, ILL., Sept. 21, 1882.

We, the undersigned, having this day received a loan of ten thousand dollars from E. C. Hegeler, for which we have given him our note to that amount, hereby bind ourselves unto him that we will not mortgage our bottle-glass works and window-glass works to any one except him during the time that the notes remain unpaid, unless giving him a first mortgage for the amount due. And we bind ourselves not to sell the above glass works, or any material part thereof, during such time. We also agree to have fire insurance on our property to the amount of ten thousand dollars transferred to him, and keep same up for his benefit.

DE STEIGER GLASS COMPANY,

PHIL. R. DE STEIGER, *Prest.*

2: The evidence shows that there was no discordance between the refusal to take a mortgage and the acceptance of the written agreement. It shows the purpose of the written agreement, and that appellant thought of reserving the right to receive a first mortgage in case the glass company should decide to mortgage its works to obtain a larger running capital ; or, secondly, in case any other creditor of the glass company should attempt to force it to give a mortgage. The evidence also shows the probability that appellant wanted definitely to reserve the right to demand a mortgage in case the statements made to him by the glass company at the time of his making the loan to it hastily, and without security, should be untrue

(Petition for Rehearing, continued.)

3. The words of the court, "he was willing," etc., with their context, might imply that appellant had an agreement with the glass company, that in case they were about to fail, he might be secured by mortgage before the creditors could find out the condition of the company, an implication not warranted by the evidence.

4. No secret lien was contemplated by the written agreement in any event. Appellant declined to take a secret lien when he might have done so, and thus make himself secure. That he contemplated an unfair preference in the future is incompatible with his action in declining to take a preference when he lent his money. There was no lien created by the agreement, and no publicity was necessary to be given to it for the protection of anybody. Publicity that appellant had loaned them $10,000 without security, would have enhanced their credit.

5. The judgment note given to the bank was a secret lien actually made. It has no legal or moral resemblance to the written agreement given to appellant.

6. The testimony of appellant concerning the object of the agreement was not brought to the attention of the court, although it appears in the full record of the case. The testimony appears in the stenographer's report as follows :

Q. What transpired between you and Mr. De Steiger with reference to security on this loan at the time you gave it, if anything? Tell the court just what passed between you and him on that subject.

A. Well, we spoke in a general way about it—what security he could give me and then it was spoken of —if he could perhaps give a mortgage, and then I think I mentioned myself, or he himself, if he gave a mortgage, I think I mentioned that—if he gave a mortgage it would spoil their credit in business ; and then it was spoken of that he perhaps might give a mortgage which was not recorded—the idea suggested itself—and then I concluded further and said that would not do because it would be dishonest against the public to hold a mortgage in that way without recording it.

Q. (By Eldredge for appellee.) Who said that?

(Petition for Rehearing, continued.)

A. I said so. I said, take the personal indorsement of the members of the De Steiger family to put upon the back of these notes ; and then before I gave him the money I asked him yet to give me a written promise that in case he should want to give a mortgage—should have to give a mortgage—then, before they should give it to anybody else, they should give me a first mortgage.

Q. Have you that paper?

A. (Producing Ex. L.) I think this be it.

Exhibit L offered and read in evidence.

*　*　*　*　*　*　*　*　*

Cross-examination by MR. DUNCAN.

Q. Did you ever inquire, down to the time that you made either of. these loans,—that is, either the loan of September 21st, or your loan of November 20, 1882—of either Mr. Brewster or Mr. Sutherland, or anybody connected with the First National Bank of Peru, as to whether the De Steiger Glass Company owed them anything or not?

A. I made no inquiry. I have no recollection thereof.

Q. They made no representations to you upon the subject, as to whether the De Steiger Glass Company was indebted to them or not?

A. No, sir. I had no intercourse with them, no recollection of any intercourse with them whatever.

Q. Did you ever tell the Peru bank people, or any of them, that you held this arrangement that is evidenced by this writing, upon which you were to have a first mortgage in case anything should happen?

A. No.

Q. You never communicated that fact to them?

A. No, sir ; I did not.

MR. HEGELER, recalled. (After argument had commenced.)

Q. Are you hard of hearing?

A. Yes, sir.

Q. Difficult to understand frequently? You have a difficulty of understanding what is said?

(Petition for Rehearing, continued.)

A. I overhear some. Yes, sir, but specially I don't hear all in detail what is said. I only hear in general any question.

Q: I find here in your testimony which is written out this question : "Did you ever tell the Peru bank people, or any of them, that you made this arrangement that this is evidenced by this writing upon which you were to have a first mortgage *in case anything should happen* ?" To which you made answer, "No." Is there any misapprehension?

A. I didn't hear the last words; otherwise I should have resented them on the spot.

Q. Did you have any arrangement with them by which you were to have a first mortgage *in case anything should happen ?*

A. In case anything should happen ! Nothing ; it was quite another case. In case they should need the money, and the money I was to give them was insufficient to give them running capital—that appeared when he brought in a second statement it was to amount—I think the debts were $40,000— that was the intention of it ; if he gave me those—if I gave him those $10,000, and that would not give them sufficient running capital, yet in the ordinary course of business for doing successful business, and it would apparently be or might be, or they might find it was necessary they should have a large loan or a larger amount, it would only be possible on a mortgage. I suppose he spoke at that time that he might have to get a loan of $50,000 on a mortgage. They could get sufficient running capital for their business only on a mortgage. That idea suggested itself to me as far as I recollect ; pretty distinct recollection ; then, in that case, if they should have to give such a large mortgage, in this way, in that case I should be secured on the first mortgage for myself ; that they didn't give a mortgage to anybody, and I was out.

Q. There was no arrangement for a mortgage *in case anything should happen?*

A. Never ! I would treat it with contempt ; all other arrangements, except that which appears in the paper as you have explained it here ; all what is in the paper ; that is all.

(Petition for Rehearing, continued.)

Cross-Examination by MR. DUNCAN.

Q. You took this writing that De Steiger gave you, and that he signed as part of the transaction between you and him ?

A. That is the last thing—my recollection, the last thing I got.

Q. Excuse me ; this writing that De Steiger made to you in which he agreed to give you a first mortgage and put you in ahead of anybody else, you took and kept that paper, didn't you ?

A. I have kept the paper—put me ahead of anybody else, how do you mean that ?

Q: Just what the writing says, that is all I mean.

MR. BULL. : The writing does not say any such thing.

A. In case he should have to give a larger mortgage, that is. what is meant ; we have spoken of that before, that I am confident ; we spoke of that before—that I had that writing. I am very certain that we have spoken of that before I had that meeting—that I would have to—that he would have to take a larger amount on a mortgage—larger amount to give him sufficient running capital, and in that case that was referred to, and in that case I should get it—that was meant.

As the court has made general intimations without definite specifications as to appellant's conduct, appellant is compelled, for the purpose of disproving the intimations, to study how the court came to its conclusions and to make definite specifications thereof.

From the evidence of Hegeler, it appears that appellant had to draw up a paper which stated that the De Steiger Glass Company promised that as Hegeler loaned it $10,000 without security, on its notes running one, two, three and four years,* it would not mortgage its works during that time, so as to give to any one else a preferred claim on it and its works. Does now

---

* This is an error owing to not having the papers which had been in the hands of the court since the trial of the case in Oct. 1886, about three years.—The notes were three only, and ran six, twelve and eighteen months from Sept. 21, 1882.

the paper drawn up by Hegeler have this meaning and only this ?

A superficial examination may make the reader believe that the words therein " except him," are unnecessary, and this may have caused the misapprehension of the court that Hegeler may at that time have had an understanding with De Steiger that he was to have a mortgage under certain undefined cir-cumstances. If the court will please read the De Steiger paper (Exhibit L), omitting the words " except him," the court will find that the paper seems liable to be construed to have the meaning that De Steigers will not and are not to mortgage their works to *anybody* (which words include Hegeler) during four years, *except at their own pleasure*, for the sake of their obtaining a larger running capital. To guard against this meaning Hegeler inserted the words " except him."*

The evidence shows that the circumstances at the time of drafting the paper, De Steiger had on the, or a preceding day, applied to Hegeler for a loan, being pressed for money. Upon Hegeler's request, De Steiger had written from memory a statement of their affairs, their assets and liabilities, being Exhibit C. (Abst. 16.) Hegeler had then demanded an abstract from their books. At the time Exhibit L was written De Steiger had presented the abstract of the books (Exhibit D), which showed an indebtedness much larger than he had stated from memory. This must have produced in Hegeler the uneasiness that De Steiger might have owed still more than the abstract from the books (Exhibit D) showed, in which case he would not impair his right to demand a mortgage.

8.   Appellant's idea was not that he should be a preferred creditor in case the glass company might be about to fail.   On the contrary, appellant was willing to take his chances, and did take his chances, with all unpreferred creditors.

9.   It is evident the mortgage thought of was a mortgage large enough to raise a sum sufficient to make the glass com-pany independent of credit.

---

*My recollection is that I wrote the agreement on a slip of paper which Mr. De Steiger copied.

(Petition for Rehearing, continued.)

10. That the court misconstrues this writing is evident from the opinion, where it inserts into the agreement the words "he should be notified." These words do not appear in the writing, and were not within the contemplation of appellant.

IV.

Presentation of points in support of appellant's petition for a rehearing in the matter of the conclusions drawn by the court in the following portion of the opinion:

"It would certainly be difficult to condemn the transaction between appellee and the glass company, without also pronouncing that of appellant fraudulent; but we know no rule of law, or business, which condemns either."

1. There is no similarity of action between the two cases. Appellant declined a secret lien while appellee accepted one.

2. Appellant declined to occupy the position of a preferred creditor; appellee demanded and accepted that position.

3. The secret lien given to appellee was to the prejudice and misleading of other creditors of the glass company. The agreement given to appellant could not be to the prejudice of anybody.

4. As the purposes of the respective transactions were unlike, so the consequences were different. The action of appellant did not result in benefit to himself nor injury to others. The reverse was the case as to the action of appellee.

5. In drawing a moral parallel not warranted by the evidence, the court may unwillingly do an injury to appellant more serious than the mere loss of the money involved in the suit.

6. While the opinion disclaims any intention to condemn the transaction assumed by the court between appellant and the glass company, it likens the transaction to the action of the bank, and thereby makes a comparison highly injurious to appellant.

(*Petition for Rehearing, continued.*)

V.

Presentation of points in support of appellant's petition for a rehearing in the matter of the conclusions drawn by the court in the following portion of the opinion:

"It must be admitted that if the averment that appellee '*agreed to conceal the same, and to allow said glass company to retain the full control of the property, free from any record or known lien,*,*and that in pursuance of such agreement, it did consent,*' etc., was stricken out of the bill, it would be demurrable for want of equity appearing on its face.

. "There is not a particle of evidence in the record to support that averment, nor is it relied upon in the argument as being essential to complainant's cause. * * * There is no pretense that there was any agreement to conceal its claim against the glass company, much less that any such agreement was made for the purpose of enabling the company to obtain credit from others."

1. There is no evidence that the president of the bank said to the president of the glass company: "In consideration of the giving of these judgment notes to us, we agree to conceal them;" but that such was the understanding must necessarily be inferred from the facts proved.

The bank refused to take a mortgage on the *express grounds of publicity* and accepted the judgment notes on the *express grounds of secrecy.* How could any argument be more clear and explicit? The arrangement was perfectly understood and mere promises would have been but an idle ceremony. Their minds had met, and that is the gist of an agreement.

2. But this court has frequently said that positive admission of fraud, or of a fraudulent intent, are not to be expected, and many things are indeed fraudulent as to third parties which are not fraudulent as between the original parties.

3. We think it must be error to require us to prove that the parties by *words* expressed a fraudulent intent when we have proved *facts* which establish it.

4. In appellant's original argument cases quite similar to the one at bar are cited, where it was held immaterial that the

(Petition for Rehearing, continued.)

parties had no fraudulent intent in the concealment ; if the concealment did, in fact, operate as a fraud on future creditors.

5. Judgment notes given in cases of financial embarrassment are fraudulent in case concealment by both maker and payee is an essential condition coupled therewith at the time of execution; that is, the concealment of the indebtedness by both debtor and creditor is in fact the fraudulent part. The judgment clause is for the sole purpose of making the conspiracy effective.

* *

[Head VI. omitted. It refers to a technical point of practice in error.]

* *

VII.

Presentation of points in support of appellant's petition for a rehearing in the matter of the conclusions drawn by the court in the following portion of the opinion :

" We know of no rule of law or business to condemn the transaction either of appellant or of appellee."

1. Appellant insists that the transaction which the court assumes took place between appellant and the glass company, was fraudulent. If the glass company had found it was insolvent and came and notified appellant, and agreed or had previously agreed to keep running until appellant could get a mortgage on record, even though the delay had been for a single day only, then for such single day the glass company would have deceived its creditors and appellant be in collusion with it.

2. It may be said that the glass company might have had the private thought, during that single day, to reimburse the creditors it was deceiving, but that does not make the deed undone.

3. It may be said there might be an understanding that the instant the glass company found, or came to the conclusion, it was bankrupt, its first thought and action should be to make appellant a preferred creditor, so that there was no time re-

(Petition for Rehearing, continued.)

quired for preparing and recording the mortgage. In that case the glass company would, of necessity, have had to secrete such a supposed understanding. It would have constantly asked men to work for it and asked persons to sell it goods on credit impressing the belief upon them that it could and would pay them, while internally saying that it made these men give credit under a peril which it kept concealed from them, and in such deception appellant would have been a participant.

4. At the same time the bank bought from the De Steiger Glass Company the fictitious drafts upon Munn and others, and debited their " Bills Payable " account and credited them to the De Steiger Glass Company, the bank lost all claim upon the glass company therefor, so far as the public is concerned. A debt can have remained only to such extent as the law may recognize as existing between two persons jointly occupied in an unlawful transaction.

In this view, together with the view that judgment notes secretly held in cases of approaching insolvency are fradulent, appellant filed his bill of complaint in the Circuit Court.

5. Counsel for appellee say, on page 16 of this brief: " The $14,500 Mr. Hegeler loaned the De Steiger Glass Company, no doubt, added to their appearance of being men of ample means. Shall it therefore be said he designed to, or did, defraud other creditors? Certainly not."

But if Mr. Hegeler under such circumstances knowingly allowed the De Steiger Glass Co. to represent to the public, or other creditors, that all the property in their possession was their own and free from incumbrance, he would have participated in such deception. Much more would this be the case if Hegeler had been their banker who is understood to be always watching his customers' proceedings and particularly so when he believes them to be embarrassed. A banker is the financial sponsor of his customer.

The honorable judge who tried this case below said in concluding: " It is a matter of regret that by this hard advantage not only Mr. Hegeler, but a number of laboring men are liable to lose their demands, yet the validity and priority of liens thus obtained has been too often upheld to be now changed

(Petition for Rehearing, continued.)

by anything less than a legislative enactment." Will the court
also, in our case uphold such opinion?

VIII.

CONCLUSION.

Appellant respectfully suggests to the court that owing to
the death of Mr. Bull, the senior counsel on his side, who had
the principal management of it, and who was familiar with
the evidence and circumstances, the management of appellant's
interest was thrown upon Mr. Strawn, surviving partner, who
was uninformed as to the points which appellant particularly
wished to urge in this court. On the 5th of March, 1889, appellant received a letter from Mr. Strawn, to the effect that he
forwarded a copy to appellant of his brief, which would have to
be filed on the then to-morrow, and that after the brief for the
other side was filed, appellant would have an opportunity to file
a reply brief, containing any additional suggestions that might
be necessary, and asking that such suggestions be forwarded.
Appellee's brief was forwarded by mail to appellant, March 13..

On the 15th of March, 1889, appellant wrote a letter
to Messrs. Brewer and Strawn, saying : " I received appellee's
brief and I wish an answer to be given to the remarks of
counsel on pages 27 and 28." On the 16th of March, appellant
received a letter from Messrs. Brewer and Strawn saying :
" Your case with the Peru bank has been called and taken
under advisement by the Supreme Court and the time for
further argument is closed." This did not allow any time for
appellant to present the points he desired to present in answer
to the injurious comparisons and suggestions contained in the
brief of appellee, which comparisons not being contradicted in
the reply brief had probably led the court to adopt them as
justified by the testimony, while the testimony completely contradicted them.

Believing that the Supreme Court wrote the opinion
under a misapprehension, and that the court would never treat

(Petition for Rehearing, continued.)

lightly the character of an American citizen, nor of any man, appellant respectfully asked a consideration of this case and particularly of the opinion filed therein.

Respectfully submitted,

M. M. TRUMBULL, and

BREWER & STRAWN,

Solicitors for Appellant.

(End of Petition for Rehearing.)

PART II.

The Supreme Court after the full information and suggestions of my petition for rehearing made at first only some very unimportant alterations in the verbiage of the obnoxious clause and in their amended opinion filed Oct. 19, 1889, left the body of the same to stand in substantially all its insulting import. Their amended language was as follows :

" Months after the transactions between appellee and the company appellant according to his own testimony declined or at least consented not to take mortgage security because it would injure its credit. He refused to take a mortgage and withhold it from record because he thought that would be dishonest against the public, but he was willing to and did make an agreement with Mr. De Steiger in case the company desired to give a mortgage on its property he should be notified and have a first mortgage. It would certainly be difficult to condemn the transaction between appellee and the glass company complained of without also comdemning that of appellant. We know of no rule of law or business by which either should be pronounced fraudulent or immoral and no reflection upon the honesty or fair dealing of appellant is hereby made."

THE OFFENSIVE CLAUSE CHANGES PLACE.

However before the publication of the bound volume of the reports of their decisions which contains my case, the Supreme Court has seen fit to expunge from their opinion the part that expressed their adoption of the offensive insinuation of the lawyer of the bank, but as it would seem they would not abandon the publication of the same altogether, and so instead of embodying the insinuation in the opinion, it has been inserted in the report of. the points made by the lawyer of the bank.   As published in the advance sheets the report of my case did not notice this as a point made by said lawyer.

This alteration by the Supreme Court of their opinion does not nullify the wanton injury which the publication of the former opinions have done to me, and which the insertion of the scandalous insinuation in the report of the points made by the lawyer of the bank has perpetuated.

In the bound volume one may read as follows, viz.:

" (Mr. G. S. Eldredge for appellee.)

*   *   *   *   *   *   *

" Hegeler made his loan to the glass company upon the "stipulation that he should have the first lien by a mortgage on " the property of the company when the exigency should occur " for its execution," etc.

· Mr. Eldredge, the lawyer of the bank, however, makes the alleged point in his. brief in the language following, viz.:

·   " Mr. Hegeler said he made these loans upon the faith of "the written representation made by De Steiger as president of "the glass company evidenced by exhibits C and D.   The last "exhibit (D) Mr. Hegeler says he received before he paid over "the money.   The particular attention of the Court is called to "his direct and cross examination.   Mr. Hegeler, it appears, " *declined to take a mortgage* as security but insisted upon the " personal endorsement of the members of the De Steiger " family and a. written promise, to execute a first mortgage " whenever the exigencies of the situation should require it, in " the words following:

" ' La Salle, Ill., Sept. 21, 1882.   ·

" ' We the undersigned having this day received a loan of "' ten thousand dollars from E. C. Hegeler, for which we have "' given our note to that amount, hereby bind ourselves unto him "' that *we will not mortgage our bottle-glass works and window-* "' *glass works to any one except him during the time that the* "' *notes remain unpaid unless giving him a* FIRST MORTGAGE "' *for the amount due.*   And we also bind ourselves not to sell

"" the above glass works or any material part thereof during such
"" time. We also agree to have fire insurance on our property
"" to the amount of ten thousand dollars transferred to him and
"" keep the same up for his benefit.

"" De Steiger Glass Co.
"" Phil. R. De Steiger, President.'

"So it will be seen that this loan was made upon the ex-
"press stipulation that he should have the first lien by way of
"mortgage on the property of the De Steiger Glass Co. when
"the exigency should occur for its execution."

By thus quoting only a part of Mr. Eldredge's brief upon
this matter and omitting to give the part that exposes his
arts of misstatement, the Report of the Supreme Court leads
the reader to believe that the counsel of the bank made an
actual point *on the basis of a bona fide analysis of the testimony*
to the effect that I was myself in collusion with the glass
company against the public. Whereas in fact Mr. Eldredge
in his brief made an *insinuation* to that effect.

Thus the Supreme Court Report publishes a libel against
me.

CRITICISM OF THE LEGAL POINTS OF THE DECISION.

The Supreme Court referring to the averment of my
bill, that the glass company "agreed to conceal the same and
to allow said glass company to retain the full control of the
property free from any recorded or known lien ; that in pursuance of such agreement said First National Bank of Peru,
with the intention of allowing said glass company to obtain
new and future credit elsewhere and to defraud its creditors,
did keep concealed," says, "It must be admitted that if the
same was stricken out of the bill it would be demurrable on its
face for want of equity." That is to say, if all the other allegations of the bill were admitted to be true and this one were
omitted, the complainant would have no case entitling him to
any relief in equity. By implication it appears that the bill
would be maintainable if the proof sustained that averment.

From this they go on to declare—

1st. That "no particle" of evidence supports that averment.

2nd. That "no evidence" even "tends to prove" any "acts or declarations by the bank calculated to induce me to give credit" to the glass company.

3rd. That "nothing" shows anywhere against the "honest belief" of the bank that the glass company would overcome its embarrassment, and pay its debts *if its credit could be maintained.*

The circumstances urged in support of the controlling averment, the court indirectly avoids considering by claiming that the argument of my counsel proceeded throughout upon the "contrary" proposition that the "bank took and held its notes under *circumstances* that made its conduct operate as a fraud upon others," and then they proceed as though circumstantial evidence was of no avail to prove fraud.

IDENTITY OF THE "AVERMENT" AND THE "PROPOSITION."

The "averment" referred to, and the "proposition" argued, are one and the same thing in substance, stated in different terms; and if the "proposition" is established by the "circumstances," so also is the "averment" of an agreement to conceal.

The terms, "to defraud its creditors" in said averment "and as a fraud upon others" used by the court, alike state, not a fact, but a conclusion to be drawn from the facts proved, and the "circumstances" alluded to can only be those recited in the averment.

The court holds that a creditor of an insolvent has the right to take judgment notes and conceal them and to allow the insolvent to retain full control of his property free from recorded or known lien, but has not the right to agree to do so. That is to say, one can have a right to do a thing which he can not rightfully make an agreement to do.

The opinion also takes the same ground with reference to the intention of the parties. What can be the nature of the thing or act which one can rightfully do but not rightfully have the intention of doing?

The court in effect requires the "intention" and the "fraud" to be directly proved, and does not consider that both are legally inferrable from the facts which are either admitted or not disputed. These things are seldom if ever provable by direct evidence, but are established as conclusions drawn from proved facts.

THE FACTS ESTABLISHED.

The following facts of said averment are established. (1) The bank knew the glass company was insolvent prior to and at the time of taking the judgment notes. (2) The bank did conceal the judgment notes. (3) The bank did allow the glass company to retain full control of the property without any known or recorded lien. (4) The bank expected the glass company would obtain future credit elsewhere. (5) The bank did delay in entering up judgment on the notes for over eleven months after they became due. (6) The bank did then enter up judgment with the express purpose of defeating all other claims, or, in other words, for the purpose of grasping all the unincumbered assets of the glass company to pay its own debt before any others.

The law is settled that an unrecorded mortgage is no effectual against the rights of others ; in other words, that the relation of creditor and debtor as to the particular property described in a mortgage in the possession of the mortgagor must be made public in order to be not fraudulent as to third parties.

It is also well settled that as against the rights of the public a recorded chattel mortgage is unavailing to protect past due notes secured thereby, the policy of the law being that it is fraudulent as to the public to permit personal property to remain in the possession of the owner with an outstanding *and matured* right of defeasance in another.

MAINTAINING THE CREDIT OF THE BANK.

In the original opinion the court uses this language:

" There is nothing in the bill, and certainly nothing in the " evidence, to show that at the time appellee took its notes and " refused to take mortgage security, it did not honestly believe, " that notwithstanding the insolvency of the glass company, it . " would, if its credit could be maintained, successfully recover " from its embarrassment, continue business and pay all its debts."

1. What is here predicated generally of the transaction is that a creditor may know the debtor to be insolvent and yet take a preference, if he honestly believes the credit of the

debtor can be maintained and he by continuing in business can pay all his debts. No notice is taken of the fact that the bank delayed taking judgment after the paper was due, and that the amount of the note was sufficient to drive the company into liquidation.

2. It is not intimated by what means the credit is to be maintained, but left to be inferred that a secretly preferred creditor may help maintain the credit of an insolvent without loss to himself in case of failure to maintain the credit.

Postponement of payment of a past due obligation of an insolvent debtor by one of his creditors, on a private agreement which would injure the credit, if made public, should have been declared fraudulent as to other creditors in case of failure.

The secrecy of the preference during the period in which the credit is maintained by the help of the creditor, yields a necessary inférence of fraud within the contemplation of both the debtor and creditor under such circumstances, and should be declared a conclusive presumption of fraud.

The creditor who thus postpones the collection of his claim against an insolvent debtor upon a judgment note, giving him the right to enter up judgment at his option, intentionally aids the debtor in obtaining further credit, to the extent to which his delay gives color to solvency and the appearance of business prosperity.

If the law permits a creditor under such circumstances to help maintain the credit of an insolvent debtor to the extent of concealing a preference at the creditor's option, it is wrong. The relation indicated should be declared fraudulent as to other creditors in case of failure. Credit given to a debtor upon a preference under circumstances where it would injure the credit of the debtor if the preference were made public, is fraudulent as to the other creditors of the debtor in case the enforcing of the preference results in producing a failure of the debtor in business.

The appearance of wealth or business prosperity with a private agreement of preference, or for a preference under the circumstances indicated, is fraudulently deceptive as to the public, and especially fraudulent is the possession of property by an insolvent, with an outstanding matured right of defeasance in another.

What has the honest (*i. e.*, real) belief of the bank to do with the case ? Does the Supreme Court mean to imply that the end may justify the means, and that a transaction is honest or fraudulent according to its success or failure?

And why may not the implied argument of the Supreme Court be applied to other cases like an unrecorded mortgage or a sale without change of possession?

HOW WAS THE CREDIT OF THE GLASS CO. TO BE MAINTAINED?

Taking it for granted that the bank "honestly believed that the company would recover from its embarrassment if its credit could be maintained," did the court stop to consider the full import of the words "if its credit could be maintained." *By what process could or was its credit to be maintained after the judgment note had been given ?* No one would then with knowledge of this fact trust the company to the extent of a single dollar. Neither the company nor the bank could thereafter maintain the credit without deceiving others with whom the glass company might deal. The bank could safely count upon the probability that no one would inquire of it. The acceptances were still held and renewed. The question with the bank and the company was: How shall we induce others dealing with the company to believe that the company is not so largely in debt as it actually is and that it owns the plant and personal property in its possession. This is the foundation of credit. That the appearance of wealth by the company was false and deceptive is without doubt. That the bank was aware of the situation is also without doubt. That the bank expected that the company would get credit upon the false and deceptive appearance can not be doubted. It knew that the company could not get credit except upon the false appearance or by making false answer to inquiries concerning its affairs.

The company did actually misrepresent its affairs to me, for the purpose of obtaining credit. We therefore have the well laid plan for misrepresentation and proof of one instance of misrepresentation by which the company obtained $14,500, which is followed shortly after by the action of the bank in entering judgment. The conclusion that it was in collusion with the company and connived at its false representations is irresistible.

The judgment notes were not made for the purpose of security *alone*, but to enable the bank to help maintain the credit of the glass company with less risk than otherwise *in case of failure*, to make the bank safer *in case of failure*. The agreement, to conceal was implied ; the bank refused a mortgage on the express ground of publicity and took the judgment notes on the express ground of secrecy. It was the purpose of both to maintain the credit and protect the bank *in case of failure;* both knew the first object would be defeated by disclosure.

THE CONTRAST BETWEEN MY CASE AND THAT OF THE BANK.

The strictly personal imputations involved in the language of the Supreme Court in the clause of their opinion that was finally dropped as coming from the court but stated as one of the prominent points made by the counsel for the appellee, I will hereafter deal with. Here however I will show how utterly groundless and bad as mere law and logic that insinuation is. Not only were my interests, motives and intentions absolutely different from those of the bank, but also the information upon which I proceeded and the natural inferences derived therefrom.

The information with which I was supplied concerning the financial condition of the glass company showed it to be the owner of property very much more than sufficient to pay all its debts. It is not pretended, has never been suggested, and can not be argued, that I believed or had any reason to believe that the glass company was unworthy of credit or that it purposed or was inclined to give preferences to one creditor over another. Upon such information no suggestion could arise in my mind that the interests of any creditor could be endangered or even disfavored by my transaction. The ordinary and natural inference would rather be that the interests of creditors would be promoted since the glass company would be supplied with a large sum of ready cash.

But the bank was intimately acquainted with the precarious financial condition of the glass company. The bank knew that the glass company was insolvent and compelled to resort to all sorts of devices to maintain its credit. The bank knew that if the public should learn the condition of the glass company as it was known to the bank, the glass company would at once be regarded as utterly unworthy of credit. The bank must have known that the glass company proposed to contract debts and borrow money from others after giving the judgment notes to the bank. The bank knew that in order to do this the glass company would be compelled to, and would misrepresent its financial condition in ways similar to that practiced upon me. The bank must have known that ignorance of the existence of its judgment notes would be an indispensable condition for the success of any effort that the glass company might make, that involved its credit. The bank knew that the interests of all existing unsecured creditors as well as the interests of all who might give credit to the glass company without taking good security, would be and remain in great jeopardy and might eventually be wholly sacrificed as a consequence of its transaction.

I lent a large sum of ready cash which increased the resources of the glass company to the extent of its amount. The bank had already parted with its money. The resources of the glass company were not, as in my case, increased, but on the very contrary they were almost as a whole placed at the mercy of the bank. My transaction had no need whatever of secrecy, but its publication in full while it might have caused an inquiry into the affairs of the glass company would upon close examination have affected its credit favorably. No secrecy could have been contemplated. The transaction of the bank, if published, would have operated to have closed both the glass company and the bank at once. Secrecy was of vital importance to both, and the very reason why the stipulations to that effect were not put in express terms was the open absurdity of verbally promising one another to conceal those things which each knew the other to be above all things anxious to conceal.

No interest or motive beyond mere good will can be imputed to me for desiring not to impair the credit of the glass company. Had I thought its credit in need of support, I would either have refused to lend, or I would have taken real security before I parted with my money. The bank had every selfish interest and motive for supporting and fostering the credit of the glass company. The very existence of the bank hung upon the maintenance of the credit of the glass company and the conduct of the bank in reference to the credit of the glass company was prompted solely by its own selfish interests and motives.

I respected the credit of the glass company, refused to take a present mortgage to remain unrecorded, waived a present mortgage to be recorded, and took the simple promise of the glass company not to (sell or) mortgage its property without first giving me a mortgage for my debt. The bank also regarded the credit of the glass company and declined any mortgage, taking in lieu of it the judgment notes.

I acted on information favorable to the credit of the company, against my own interests. The bank acted on full information that fully impeached the credit of the company, in pursuit solely of its own interests.

THE INSINUATION.

In its original opinion the Supreme Court said:

"Months after the transaction between appellee and the "company, appellant, according to his own testimony, declined, "or at least consented not to take mortgage security, because it "would 'spoil their credit.' He refused to take a mortgage "and withhold it from record, because he thought that would "'be dishonest against the public,' but he was willing to and did "make an agreement with Mr. De Steiger that in case the com- "pany desired to give a mortgage he should be notified and have "a first mortgage. It would certainly be difficult to condemn "the transaction between appellee and the glass company with- "out also pronouncing that of appellant fraudulent (and he is "the only one here complaining); but we know of no rule of "law or business which condemns either."

This language was altered slightly in the amended opinion filed Oct. 19, 1889, so as to read thus, viz.:

"Months after the transactions between, appellee and the
"company, appellant, according to his own testimony, declined,
' or at least consented not to take mortgage security because it
"would injure its credit. He refused to take a mortgage and
"withhold it from record because he thought that would be dis-
"honest against the public, but he was willing to and did make
"an agreement with Mr. De Steiger in case the company desired
"to give a mortgage on its property he should be notified and
"have a first mortgage. It would certainly be difficult to con-
"demn the transaction between appellee and the glass company
"complained of without also condemning that of appellant. We
"know of no rule of law or business by which either should be
"pronounced fraudulent or immoral and no reflection upon. the
"honesty or fair dealing of appellant is hereby made."

By this language in both forms of opinion the Supreme
Court insinuates that according to my testimony I supposed
that the De Steigers, on finding themselves hopelessly bankrupt, would naturally resolve to give to some friend of theirs a
mortgage for their own benefit.

They insinuate that the glass company and myself had an
understanding in regard to this supposed project on its part
and in regard to its precarious financial condition. They insinuate that I was ready to conceal from others the condition of
the glass company, ready to favor its dishonest designs against
others and ready to support an unmerited credit for it. They
insinuate that I took "Exhibit L" with these ideas especially
in mind. They insinuate that my refusal to take an unrecorded
mortgage on the ground that it would be dishonest against the
public was a piece of pretense and hypocrisy.

In order to give more color to their insinuations, they
say that I made an "*agreement*" with De Steiger that whenever the glass company "*desired*" I was to be "*notified*"
and have a first mortgage. Notice the subtle design of the
language used. Mark the office and effect of the words
"agreement," "desired," and "notified" as the Supreme Court
has combined them with its other expressions. What is intended to be conveyed thus but that I was privy to the "de-
sires" of the glass company and had so good an "understanding" with Mr. De Steiger and he with me in respect to the

occasion proper for my first mortgage, that he was, as it were, to stand on guard and "notify" me when the anticipated occasion should arrive?

And all this appears, so the Supreme Court say, "according to my own testimony."

Now at least at the time of the filing of the amended opinion the Supreme Court must have known better than to make the assertion that any such thing or things appear "according to my own testimony." By my petition for a rehearing the Supreme Court was shown that my testimony was precisely to the very contrary effect. (See my testimony printed on pp. 24–27.) So also in regard to the other reckless assertion that I was to be "*notified*" by the De Steigers when it should become proper for me to have a first mortgage. In my petition for a rehearing I pointed out the groundlessness' of this assertion, that the words did not appear in "Exhibit L," and that they were not contemplated by me.

When such misrepresentations are made by the Supreme Court why should it not be said that they are characteristic marks of the spirit that governed its action and expression? Why should it not be said that they are chargeable with plain prevaricat on and with perverting the evidence for sinister purposes against me?

THE INSINUATION GROUNDLESS.

It is not possible to construe "Exhibit L" to mean any promise to give me any special favor. Indeed it is but the bare promise of the company not to defraud me by cutting off my recourse on their property. It did not imply that the glass company was to give me any mortgage whatever, save only in the one case (if it should occur) that the glass company should be about to mortgage its property to some one else than me.

By the terms of "Exhibit L," which was drawn up in close relation with Mr. De Steiger's statement "Exhibit C" and the balance sheet, "Exhibit D," I was to have a first mortgage from the glass company in case they should mortgage their property.

Now under what circumstances must any case that can be supposed in the matter be imagined ? So far as I can see there are only three cases.

1st. Some creditor of the glass company might become uneasy and demand payment or mortgage security, threatening suit in case his demands were not complied with.

In this case the glass company would have shown the importuning creditor the balance sheet which they showed to me, or rather a similar one. They would also have said to the threatening creditor, " If you insist on a mortgage from us we are bound to Mr. Hegeler to give him a first mortgage for the $10,000 which he loaned to us without real security on our promise to him not to mortgage our property without first giving him a first mortgage. Had then the threatening creditor still urged for his mortgage and in consequence the glass company had given to me the first mortgage for my $10,000, and then to the threatening creditor a second mortgage, the other creditors would have been in the condition as follows:

As by the balance sheet shown to me the material on hand and the stock alone was nearly sufficient to pay off all the indebtedness of the glass company, and the real estate and works were scheduled in the balance sheet at $88,930, incumbered with only the old mortgage of $5,000 on the window-glass house scheduled at $9,000, which mortgage I was to take up as an investment, the glass company by going into liquidation could with the aid of only $2,110, to be derived from the sale or mortgage of their real estate, pay all debts.

2nd. This is the main case under consideration in drawing " Exhibit L " and is that the glass company would see the advisability of mortgaging their whole plant for a sufficient sum to enable it to do a cash business—say $35,000, besides the $5,000 window-house mortgage, the old mortgage which I was taking up as an investment, in which case it would either give me a first mortgage, or as would be more likely, would pay off my notes.

3d. This is the case which the Supreme Court insinuated against me.

The Supreme Court as a necessary conclusion from their

opinion, regards it as the ordinary, natural supposition that the De Steigers on finding themselves hopelessly bankrupt would resolve to give to some friend of theirs a wholesale mortgage of their plant for the purpose of holding the same for their benefit, and the Supreme Court insinuate that I supposed likewise and had it in mind when I requested them to give me the paper "Exhibit L " in order to have a first mortgage before this contemplated fraudulent mortgage.

The Supreme Court seem actually to believe that I would have loaned $10,000 to De Steiger on no security but the personal endorsements of the De Steiger family yet believing that they would thus treat their creditors.

THE MOTIVES OF THE INSINUATION.

Now what account can be given why the Supreme Court acted as it did?

Mr. Eldredge in referring to " Exhibit L," and the circumstances of its passing, says:

"So it will be seen that this loan was made upon the "express stipulation that he should have the first lien by way "of a mortgage on the property of De Steiger Glass Company, "*when the exigency should occur for its execution;*" meaning to imply and suggest that there was some evidence to the effect that " Exhibit L " had reference to the giving me a first mortgage in case the glass company should be in straits and propose and be about to arrange its property to the disadvantage of its creditors at large. This charge is not directly made, it is *insinuated.*

Webster thus defines the insinuation as related to the innuendo or direct charge, " An insinuation turns on no double "use of language, but consists in artfully winding into the "mind imputations of an injurious nature without making any "direct charge, and is, therefore, justly regarded as one of the "basest resorts of malice and falsehood."

This insinuation of the lawyer of the bank, the Supreme Court seized upon with that light esteem with which they seem to regard the good names of suitors. They took up " Exhibit L," out of its intimate connection with the statement made from memory by De Steiger (" Exhibit C," see p. 4) and the balance sheet (see p. 4). The fact that my leading counsel, Mr. Bull, had died, and that the briefs were filed in close succession at the last moment did not secure their attention. They find for my reply brief, nothing but a copy of the opinion of the Appellate Court and no repelling of the insinuation of Mr. Eldredge. They apparently do not look into the opinion of the Appellate Court to see if the charge against me is there made, nor into that of the Circuit Court which tried the case, but all unsupported by even any attempt at proof as they find the insinuation of Mr. Eldredge to be, they themselves from the abstract of my testimony, echo and dress up the same insinuation, and thereby impute to me that I hypocritically placed myself on high moral grounds in refusing a mortgage that was not to be recorded because "*that would be dishonest against the public*," and at the same time, I craftily schemed to accomplish essentially the same thing under cover.

Now, is it compatible with proper judicial ethics for the Supreme Court to make such an insinuation? Should they not openly have said, in case they regarded the matter as relevant to the case before them: "We find in the brief of the appellee the insinuation made that appellant obtained from the De Steiger Glass Company in the 'Exhibit L' a similar security to that which he charges as fraudulent in appellee. We find no answer to this serious charge in appellant's reply brief, and as his testimony in regard to his not wanting to spoil the credit of the glass company, as well as the meaning of 'Exhibit L,' is unclear to us, we find against him for that reason."

Had not the insinuations of the Supreme Court against me in their original opinion been repeated and persisted in after my petition for a rehearing, their original course in the matter would allow of excuses which their subsequent delinquencies forbid.

They are all men who are supposed to possess good intelligence. They would undoubtedly prefer not to have their conduct excused at the expense of the vigor of their understandings.

But after the filing of my petition for a rehearing which courteously directed their attention to my testimony (see p.

26), and fully informed them concerning the groundlessness and impropriety of the insinuations of the lawyer of the bank which they had repeated, and which also explained to them that the lack of an answer in my reply brief to his insinuations was a consequence of the death of my counsel, and after the Supreme Court instead of granting that petition for rehearing, reiterated their adopted insinuation, no excuse is imaginable that does not impeach either their intelligence or their moral integrity as faithful and dispassionate judges.

The matters insinuated against me touched not merely the recovery or loss of a sum of money, but my good name. Hence it would behoove honorable men to ascertain first of all whether or not the matters insinuated were pertinent to the issues involved in the case. If not, then the only notice fit to be taken thereof would be a rebuke to the counsel for making the insinuation. If, however, it should appear necessary to decide upon the matters involved in the insinuation, then certainly I should have had the opportunity to have met that issue. Definite charges instead of insinuations should have been required.

Or does the Supreme Court regard itself above and exempt from the observance of those rules which are recognized as binding among all men who expect to be regarded as honorable — those rules of justice all the more sacred because there is no tribunal to enforce them save the consent and reprobation of honorable men?

Does the Supreme Court regard those rules as rules which mere office-holding is privileged to dispense with?

So it would seem; and to all right thinking and right feeling the most outrageous feature of the conduct of the Supreme Court in my case is the careless, lordly superciliousness they manifest in regard to their dealings with my good name.

This spirit is specially noticeable in their evident notion that a remark like "no reflection upon the honesty and fair dealing of appellant is hereby made," is all that ought to be expected from them and ought to be taken by me as a sufficient remedy for the wrong of their still standing insinuation.

Their disclaimer that no reflection upon my honesty or fair dealing is made by them stood absolutely worthless and absurd while they reiterated and persisted in the same insinuations as at first

Moreover when at last this insinuation was dropped out of their opinion, potent persuasions seem to have existed for inserting it still in a place in the report of my case where it had not appeared in the advance sheets of the same.

SUPREME COURT ETHICS.

And yet they say that they "know of no rule of law or business by which either (transaction) should be pronounced fraudulent or immoral."

Thus according to the Supreme Court, in a case where two parties are so involved together in business that the one regards his interests as likely to be promoted by the probable projected frauds of the other, that one may, *knowingly* and intentionally and for the mere advantage of his own interests, contribute to the frauds of the other the otherwise lacking and indispensable *conditions of their success*, and to the prejudice of those defrauded, may reap his expected advantage thereby, and yet obtain the absolution of the Supreme Court of Illinois as innocent, not only of fraud but also of any kind of immorality.

This may be a fair sample of the standard of morals approved by the Supreme Court. If so a lax standard of business and law must be able to pass with them and also it may be that a lax standard of sensibility in regard to honor and good name is expected by them to obtain among those who have to deal with them.

But I have it to say very plainly that I differ with them utterly. If my conduct was truly similar to that of the bank then their comparison was merited in open, plain, honest terms, and need not have been covertly insinuated. I will not, however, say with them that I " know of no rule of law or busi-"ness by which such conduct should be pronounced fraudulent "or immoral." I say that such conduct as that of the bank and such as that which the Supreme Court *falsely* insinuate and foster against me is the conduct of swindlers and cheats, and ought to receive the reprobation of all good citizens—that it is a reproach that courts of law should not visit such conduct with their severe denunciation and endeavor to correct the injuries caused thereby.

I herewith express my thanks to the gentlemen who assisted me in preparing this pamphlet.

EDWARD C. HEGELER.

La Salle, Illinois.
August, 1890.

www.ingramcontent.com/pod-product-compliance
Lightning Source LLC
Chambersburg PA
CBHW030858260626
47169CB00008B/2593